A Note to Parents and Caregivers:

Read-it! Joke Books are for children who are moving ahead on the amazing road to reading. These fun books support the acquisition and extension of reading skills as well as a love of books.

Published by the same company that produces *Read-it!* Readers, these books introduce the question/answer pattern that helps children expand their thinking about language structure and book formats.

When sharing a book with your child, read in short stretches, pausing often to talk about the pictures and the meaning of the book. The question/answer format works well for this purpose and provides an opportunity to talk about the language and meaning of the jokes. Have your child turn the pages and point to the pictures and familiar words. Read the story in a natural voice; have fun creating the voices of characters or emphasizing some important words. And be sure to reread favorite parts.

There is no right or wrong way to share books with children. Find time to read with your child, and pass on the legacy of literacy.

Adria F. Klein, Ph.D.
Professor Emeritus
California State University
San Bernardino, California

Managing Editor: Bob Temple
Creative Director: Terri Foley
Editor: Sara E. Hoffmann
Designers: John Moldstad, Amy Bailey
Page production: Picture Window Books
The illustrations in this book were prepared digitally.

Picture Window Books
5115 Excelsior Boulevard
Suite 232
Minneapolis, MN 55416
1-877-845-8392
www.picturewindowbooks.com

Printed in the United States of America.

Library of Congress Cataloging-in-Publication Data
Dahl, Michael.
Zoodles : a book of riddles about animals /
written by Michael Dahl ; illustrated by Ned Shaw.
p. cm.—(Read-it! joke books)
ISBN 1-4048-0230-4
1. Riddles, Juvenile. 2. Animals—Juvenile humor.
I. Shaw, Ned ill. II. Title.
PN6371.5 .D358 2003
818'.602—dc21
2003004869

Zoodles

A Book of Riddles About Animals

Michael Dahl • Illustrated by Ned Shaw

Reading Advisers:
Adria F. Klein, Ph.D.
Professor Emeritus, California State University
San Bernardino, California

Susan Kesselring, M.A., Literacy Educator
Rosemount-Apple Valley-Eagan (Minnesota) School District

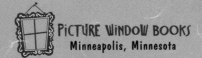

PICTURE WINDOW BOOKS
Minneapolis, Minnesota

What side of a chicken has the most feathers?

The outside.

What do chimpanzees eat for a snack?

Chocolate chimp cookies.

What kind of pigs do you find on the highway?

Road hogs.

How can you tell when it's raining cats and dogs?

When you step into a poodle.

What do you call a crab that plays baseball?

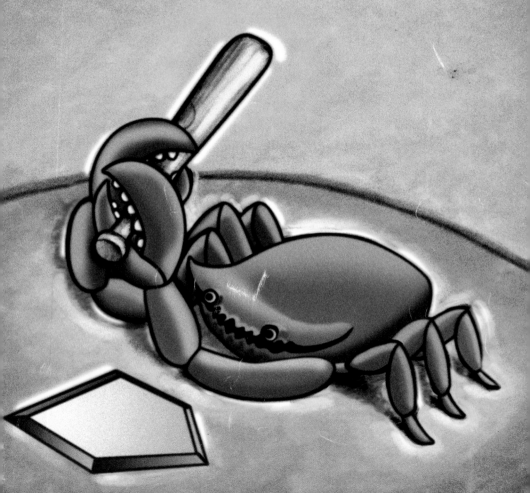

A pinch-hitter.

What happened when the bee telephoned his friend?

He got a buzzy signal.

Where do sheep go for haircuts?

The baa-baa shop.

What is a hot and noisy duck?

QUACK
QUACK
QUACK

A firequacker. 13

Why don't lobsters share their toys?

Because they're shellfish.

What kind of dog has no tail, no nose, and no fur?

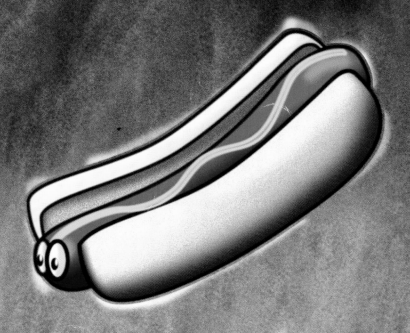

A hot dog.

What animal
talks the most?

A yak.

What school contest did the skunk win?

The smelling bee.

What pet makes the loudest noise?

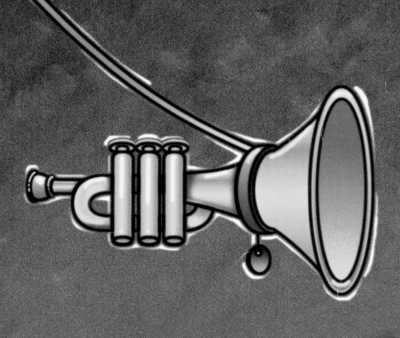

A trum-pet.

What kind of vitamin do fish need?

Vitamin sea.

What did the banana do when it saw the hungry monkey?

The banana split.

What do you call the top of a dog house?

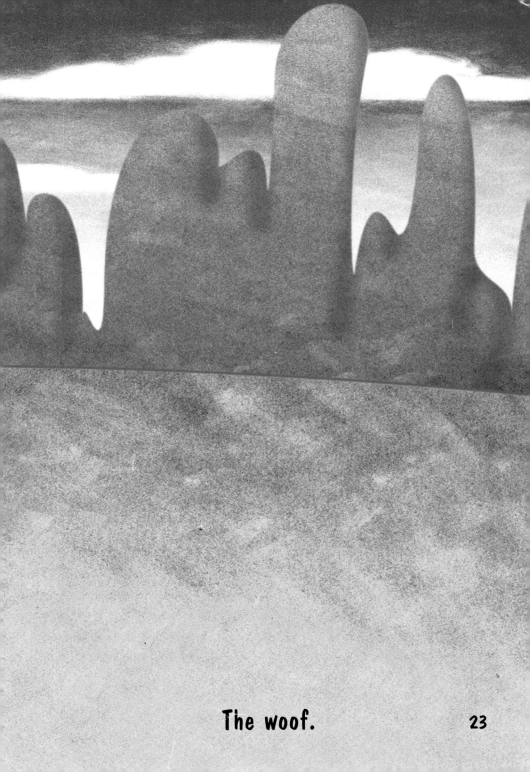

The woof.

Who steals soap from the bathroom?

The robber duckie!